W9-BNR-445

Three Thrillers from Poe, Master of Horror

based on the stories by
Edgar Allan Poe

SCHOLASTIC INC.
New York Toronto London Auckland Sydney
Mexico City New Delhi Hong Kong Buenos Aires

Cover and interior illustrations by
Clint Hansen

Contents

The Fall of the House of Usher

Is it Usher's imagination, or is his house out to get him?

An old friend, Roderick Usher, asked me to come visit right away. He was ill. I hadn't seen Usher in a long time. We had been close as boys, but there had always been a side of him I felt I didn't really know.

When I got to his house, my heart froze. Usher lived in an old stone mansion that was barely standing. It was surrounded by dead bushes, a few rotting tree trunks, and a dark moat. But the strangest of all was a long crack that zigzagged down the front of the house like a scar.

The house had been in Usher's family for hundreds of years. Maybe that was why it seemed so creepy. All the generations of Ushers had lived and died there.

I crossed the moat on a creaky bridge. Inside, the house was dark.

Feeling my way, I slowly entered the large, dimly lit room. Its windows were draped with blood-red cloth.

Just then, Roderick Usher got up from his sofa.

I had never seen a person change so much. His eyes were watery. His lips were colorless. His skin was as pale as a ghost's. And yet there was something in his expression that reminded me exactly of how he had been when we were boys.

"So good to see you, friend," Usher said, with a worried voice.

I asked what was the trouble.

"I'm suffering from an evil family disease for which there is no cure," he said. "Everything fills me with terror."

"What can I do?"

"Sit, sit. Please make yourself comfortable," said Usher.

But comfort was not possible. The walls were shadowy, and sudden gusts of wind blew through the room. The place filled me with dread.

Usher said that one other person lived in the house: his beloved sister, Madeline. She was his only living relative. But she, too, was ill.

As he spoke, Madeline passed through the back of the room. Then she disappeared into the dark.

For the next several days, I tried to lift Usher's spirits. We sat together and read books.

One day he asked, "Do you think the stone walls of this house are alive?"

I said that it might be a matter of opinion.

"They are," he said. "Unlike my sister—who is alive no more. She died last night."

My heart froze. Roderick Usher was the last of his family line.

To prepare Usher's sister for burial, we laid her in an iron casket. We slid the casket into an empty vault in the dungeon. The dungeon was right below the bedroom I was staying in.

When we shut the iron door of the vault, it made a sharp, grating sound.

That night, a storm gathered. The drapes of

my bedroom windows rustled. I began to tremble with a sense of horror I had never felt before. I heard a noise on the stairs.

It was Usher carrying a lantern.

"Have you seen the storm?" he asked.

Usher opened a window. The fury of the storm winds nearly lifted us off our feet.

Neither Usher nor I could sleep. I decided we should read a story out loud.

As I began to read, I heard a rattling sound.

It's just the wind, I told myself.

I continued to read. Just then, I heard the rattling again. Then a sharp, grating, screaming sound came from below.

Usher was facing away from me. I continued to read. The clanging and screaming got worse.

I tapped my pale friend's shoulder. He turned to me. A sickly smile quivered on his lips.

"Do you hear it?" he asked.

It sounded as though a casket was removing itself from the vault below us.

Usher cried out, "I don't know who is alive in

this house and who is dead!"

Suddenly, a gust of wind blew open the window. It drove Usher to the floor. He wrestled with some invisible force, as if a ghost were beside him—the ghost of his sister, and perhaps the ghosts of others.

At last Roderick Usher lay still.

I fled from that house. The storm outside was wild. For an instant, the night flashed bright with lightning.

Suddenly, I turned back in time to see the walls of the mansion split open. The split tore along the strange zigzag crack. Then, with a horrible groan, the dark moat swallowed the House of Usher.

The Tell-Tale Heart

Some secrets just won't keep!

I can't say how the idea first entered my brain, but once it was there, it haunted me day and night. There wasn't any reason for it. I liked the old man. He never did anything to hurt me. And I wasn't after his money.

I think it was that eye! Yes, that was it! One of his eyes looked like the eye of a vulture—pale gray with a film over it. Whenever it looked at me, my blood ran cold. I made up my mind to kill the old man and get rid of that eye forever.

I made my move slowly. Every night at midnight, I opened his door very gently, poked my head in, and shined a lantern on his vulture eye.

I did this for seven nights—every night just at midnight. But the eye was always closed, so I could not bring myself to do what I had to do. It was only his evil eye that I hated.

On the eighth night, I was even more careful than usual. But then I thought about how peacefully he slept, not even dreaming of my secret thought. And I had to laugh.

He moved suddenly. Perhaps he heard me. His room was dark, so I knew he couldn't see the door opening.

My head was already in the room. I was about to turn the lantern on. But my thumb slipped on the switch. The old man sat up in bed, crying, "Who's there?"

I kept still, not moving an inch. Finally, I heard a slight groan. I knew it was a groan of terror— terror in the face of death. I knew the terror that the old man felt and I felt sorry for him, although I laughed inside.

He must have been lying awake ever since the first small noise. He probably tried to tell himself, "It is nothing but the wind in the chimney . . . It is only a mouse crossing the floor . . . It is just a cricket."

I waited a long time, and then I turned the lantern up a little bit. I was careful. Only a single ray shot out and fell on his vulture eye.

The eye was wide open! I grew angry as I looked at it. I could see it perfectly. That dull gray eye with an ugly film over it chilled my bones.

Then I heard it—a low, dull, quick sound. It was like the sound a watch makes when it's wrapped in cotton. It was the beating of the old man's heart. It made me angrier still. But I was like a statue. I hardly breathed at all. I kept the ray of light shining on his eye. The beating of his heart grew quicker and quicker, and louder and louder.

In the dead hour of the night, in the awful silence of that old house, that noise terrified me. Yet for a few minutes longer, I stood still.

The beating grew louder, louder! Then a new fear grabbed me. The sound was so loud that a neighbor might hear it!

With a loud yell, I turned the lantern up and leaped into the room. He screamed once, only once, before I dragged him to the floor and pulled the heavy bed over him.

I smiled. The deed was almost done. For many minutes his heart beat on with a muffled sound.

Finally it stopped. The old man was dead. I removed the bed and looked at the body. I put my hand on his heart and held it there for many minutes. There was no heartbeat. His eye would not trouble me ever again.

I worked quickly but silently as I pulled up three boards from the floor. Then I slipped the old man's body into the space below and replaced the boards so well that no human eye could have found anything wrong. Ha, ha! I had done it!

Soon after I'd finished, someone knocked at the door. It was three policemen who said that a neighbor had heard a scream. I smiled and invited them in. The scream, I said, was my own. I'd had a nightmare. I told them that the old man was away in the country. I told them to search the house— search it well.

Finally, I took them into his room and asked them to sit down. I placed my chair on the floorboards above his body.

The policemen were satisfied since I seemed very much at ease.

It was almost too easy! But as we spoke, I felt myself getting pale. My head hurt and I imagined a pounding in my ears. The policemen just sat there, talking and talking. But the pounding in my ears grew louder. Finally, I had to admit the truth of it to myself. The terrible noise was not just in my head. What could it be, I wondered?

I tried talking more quickly and in a louder voice. But the sound got louder too. What could I do? It was a low, dull, quick sound. It was like the sound a watch makes when it is wrapped in cotton.

The police didn't seem to hear it, so I kept talking, even more quickly. The noise got louder.

The men kept talking. Was it possible that they did not hear it? No. They must have heard, and they knew! They were waiting for me to crack. They were mocking me in my terror.

Anything was better than this. No punishment could be worse. I couldn't stand their false smiles any longer. I had to scream—scream or die. The noise got louder, louder, louder!

"Enough!" I shrieked. "I admit it! Tear up the floor! Here! Here! It is the beating of the old man's hideous heart."

The Pit and the Pendulum

They wanted to kill him, but not quickly.

Note: This story is set near the end of the Spanish Inquisition. The Inquisition took place in Spain from 1478 to 1834. During this time, people who were accused of being enemies of the church were tortured and killed.

I was sick to death of the torture. It was better to confess. I heard the judges read my punishment. Their voices were a dreamy hum. Then, everything disappeared into darkness and silence.

When I finally woke, I could hear my heart beating in my ears. Wherever I was, it was black as night. I could see nothing.

I could barely breathe from fear. Was I to be buried alive? Or would they keep me for months in this dark dungeon?

I started feeling my way around the cell. As I moved, my mind raced. I had heard of so many evils done by this Inquisition. I knew they would kill me in some painful way, I just didn't know how or when.

I dropped a rag next to the wall. I took a hundred paces, following the wall, but I ended up back where I started, next to my rag. Next, I decided to try to walk across the round cell.

I fell flat on my face. I must have tripped. My body rested on the floor. My head rested over a hole. A wet, dirty smell rose from below.

I found a small stone and dropped it down the hole. It hit against the sides of the hole. Then it fell into water at the bottom. I was proud of myself for not falling in by accident. I crawled back to the wall. There I found a cup of water and a dish of meat. I ate, drank, and fell asleep.

When I woke, there was a dim light in the room. During my sleep, I had been tied down to a wooden board. I could only lift my head. I was so thirsty. But the water was gone.

I looked at the ceiling. There was a painted figure of Father Time, an old man with a long beard. He was holding a huge pendulum, as one sees on tall clocks. The pendulum was moving back and forth very slowly, in a very short arc.

I heard something on the floor next to me. Hundreds of huge rats had crawled out of the pit. They smelled the meat in the dish beside me. With much effort, I scared them off.

When I looked up again, the pendulum had dropped down. The sweep of its arc was wider. It swung faster than before. I could see now that a long razor was attached to the bottom of the pendulum. The whole structure was made of metal. I could hear it hiss as it swung though the air. It was getting closer.

It dropped lower, inch by inch. I slept. I woke. Days passed. Finally, it was only inches away. I could smell the metal. For a moment, I wished it would fall faster. I longed to be dead already. Then suddenly, I felt calm. I stared at the glittering death, as if it were a child's toy.

The pendulum was now swinging right above my chest. I could see that when it met my body, it would cut into my clothes, my flesh, and then my heart.

It was so close, and so loud. It shrieked like a demon as it cut through the air. I struggled, and freed my left hand.

The rats were still watching me. They had eaten most of my meat. I tried to shoo them away, but they weren't scared anymore. That's when the idea came to me. I smeared the rest of the food on the ropes that bound me.

I lay still, and the rats held back. Then, all at once, hundreds of them crawled all over me. The pendulum did not bother them at all. They squirmed on my throat. They sniffed my lips. I was almost choked by their weight. Then, I felt the ropes loosen. The rats had chewed through them.

I slid from the ropes, then away!

The pendulum was quickly pulled up through the ceiling of the chamber. I was free. But I was still trapped in my cell.

Suddenly, the walls started to glow red-hot.

They were closing in on me. They pushed me closer and closer to the pit. Burned and shaking, I soon had nowhere to stand. With a final scream, I balanced on the edge of the pit.

A loud blast sounded like trumpets! There was a hum of voices! The walls made a harsh grating, as they were drawn back! An outstretched arm caught my own, as I fell fainting into the pit. It was the arm of General Lasalle. The French army had rescued me. The Inquisition had finally been defeated by its enemies.

Edgar Allan Poe: Master of Horror

Edgar Allan Poe's life was as mysterious as the stories he wrote.

They found him lying in a Baltimore street. Nobody knew how he got there. He was barely conscious. Four days later, Edgar Allan Poe died.

He was only 40 years old. Did he die of some disease, like rabies? Was he beaten up by thugs? No one knows for sure.

When Poe died, in 1849, few people knew that he was one of America's greatest writers. He died as he had lived: poor and almost unknown.

During his short, sad life, Poe wrote some pretty scary stories. He invented the detective story and brought horror to an art form.

Searching for Clues

Poe's stories pushed the limits of creepiness. Why did he write such bizarre tales?

Poe was known among his friends as a brilliant thinker. He could captivate people for hours with his exciting, passionate talk.

Many modern experts say that Poe may have suffered from bipolar disorder. This is a disease that causes wild mood swings, from overexcited to severely depressed.

Poe had a lot of other problems too. Some were physical. Some were emotional. His life was never easy.

He was born in 1809, in Boston. His parents were struggling actors. They could barely make ends meet. Shortly after Poe turned two, his father abandoned the family.

Then his mother became ill and died, leaving behind Poe and two other small children. Poe was sent to live with John and Frances Allan. They were a wealthy couple in Richmond, Virginia.

Frances Allan could not have children of her own. She was drawn instantly to the adorable boy.

Mr. Allan, however, never fully accepted Poe. He refused to adopt the boy legally.

When Poe was five, Mr. Allan's business took the family to England. There, Poe attended the Manor House School. He remembered it as "a large, rambling Elizabethan house, in a misty-looking village of England." The school would inspire some of the remote settings of his tales.

Looking for Love

In 1820, the family returned to Richmond. Mr. Allan made life hard for young Poe. He ridiculed the boy, calling him "sulky and ill-tempered to all the family."

Craving affection, Poe fell in love with a neighbor. She was a 15-year-old girl named Elmira Royster. The two wanted to marry, but her father disapproved.

Poe left to attend college at the University of Virginia. He wrote to Elmira often. But because her father never approved of Poe, she married a wealthy businessman instead.

Poe was heartbroken. He later wrote a poem about Elmira. Most of his poems would be about lost love.

Gambling Debts

At college, Poe tried to fit in with his classmates. Most of them were wealthy like the Allans. But Mr. Allan had given Poe very little money. He could barely afford to pay for his books.

Hoping to meet expenses, he started to gamble. He piled up huge debts, which Mr. Allan refused to pay. The two fought bitterly.

Feeling unloved and mistreated, Poe left home and quit school. For a while he slept in the streets. He nearly starved.

Finally, Poe enlisted in the army because he needed food and shelter. But he dreamed of becoming a poet, and soon left military life.

Poe then went to live with his aunt, Maria Poe Clemm. She was his father's widowed sister. He called her "Muddy," and loved her as if she were his own mother.

A widowed seamstress, Muddy had two children. Eventually, Poe married her daughter, his cousin Virginia. He was 27 and she was 13!

Poe worked to support his young bride and her mother through writing and editing. He won a contest for one of his first stories. Yet he rarely got much recognition, or money, for his work.

Poe lost one editing job after another. Usually it was because of his wild behavior. He made enemies by writing cruel reviews of other writers' books, calling their writing "worthless," or "sickening."

The Raven

But Poe kept writing—horror tales, detective stories, and poems.

In 1845, his poem, *The Raven*, finally won him fame. Fans called him "the Raven" because he dressed in black.

Still, Poe could not work his way out of poverty. He and Virginia and Muddy moved from boardinghouse to boardinghouse. Sometimes they couldn't afford firewood. They would burn their furniture to stay warm.

At age 20, Virginia became ill with tuberculosis. She lay in bed shivering, warmed only by her husband's tattered overcoat.

Virginia died at the age of 24. Grief-stricken, Poe sneaked out at night to cry at her grave. But he knew that if he and Muddy were to survive, he would need to find work—or a wealthy woman to marry.

Poe learned that his childhood sweetheart, Elmira, was now a widow. And she was rich. He rushed to Richmond to ask if she would marry him. Elmira consented. A second chance at happiness finally seemed within his reach.

But there was no happy ending after all. A week later Poe was dead.